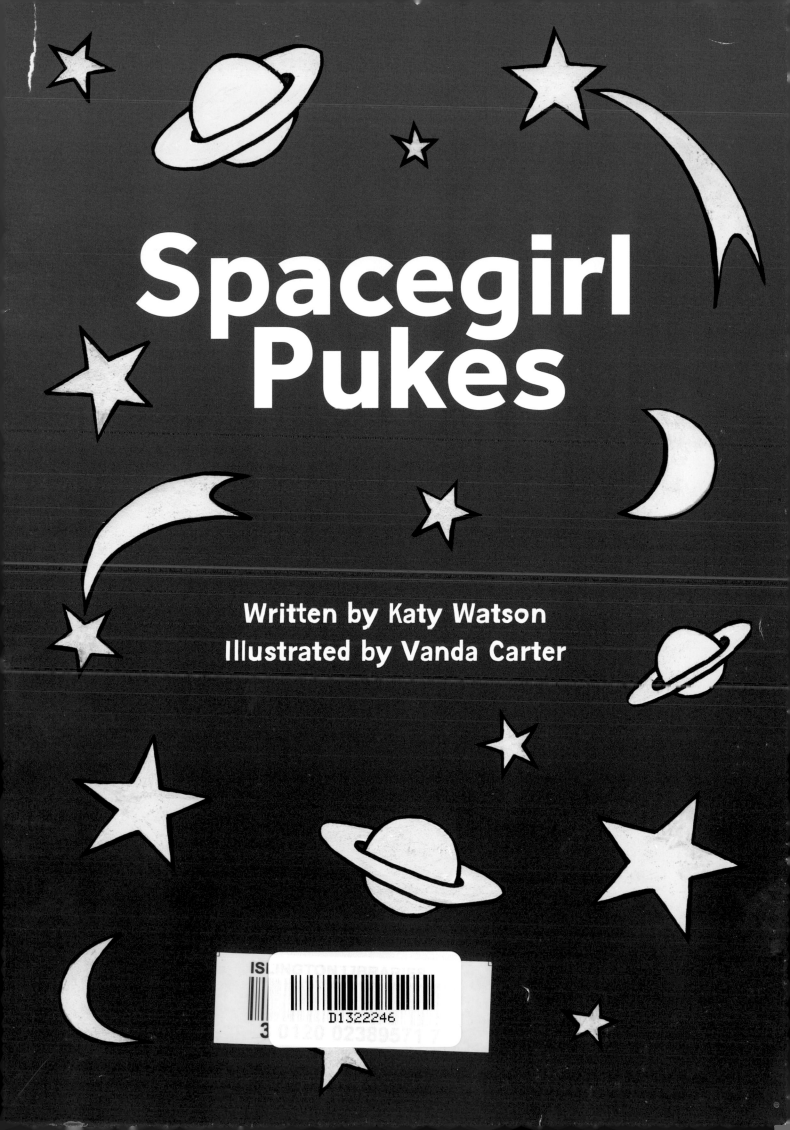

Spacegirl Pukes

Written by Katy Watson
Illustrated by Vanda Carter

Spacegirl was all ready for take-off on her latest mission when suddenly she felt a pain in her tummy.

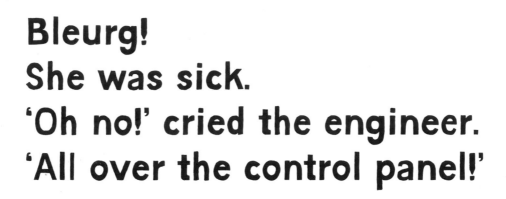

Bleurg!
She was sick.
'Oh no!' cried the engineer.
'All over the control panel!'

TIONS: 09.08.40 / WEATHER CONDITIONS: 09.08.43 / WEATH
LIGHT BREEZE. TEMPERATURE 16°C. DRY AND SUNNY DAY

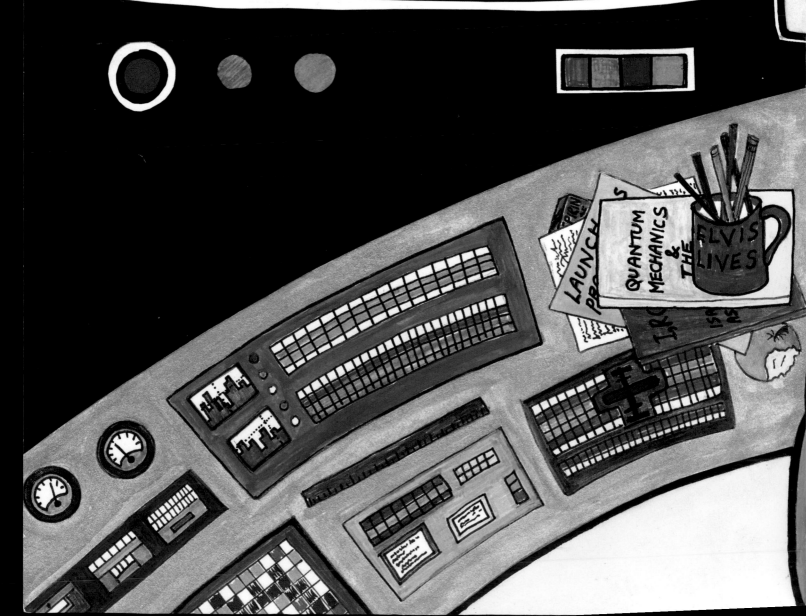

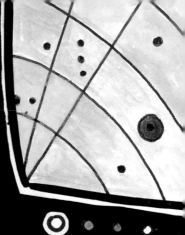

GALACTIC POSITIONING — ON
ENGINE STATUS — PRIMED
FUEL STATUS — EMPTY
LIFE SUPPORT — OPERATIONAL
TURBO BOOSTER — PRIMED
WARP DRIVE — ON

.591003.671298
1583147.008327
.2412911.580461
9881042.663904
.634709.514823
.317884.796190
.249673.141099
.751429.110703
.417921.150561

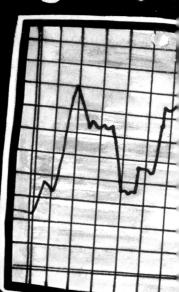

Spacegirl started to cry. She hadn't been expecting to be sick. Mummy Loula hugged her. Now there was sick on both of them.

Mummy Neenee got some tissues and wiped them both.

'Oh dear,' said Mummy
Neenee, 'you must have
caught that bug from your
friend Starboy.'

At home, Mummy Loula and Mummy Neenee tucked Spacegirl up in their bed. They put a bucket next to the bed in case she was sick again. Poor Spacegirl!

Then Mummy Neenee said, 'Oh no!'
Bleurg!

She was sick in the bucket. Then
Mummy Loula was sick as well.
Bleurg!

Poor mummies!
Poor Spacegirl!

They all got into bed together.

Then Trotsky the cat came in. He made a funny little coughing noise. K-k-ka! And he was sick on the floor.

They all felt really ill.

When Spacegirl was feeling better she went back to the rocket.

One of the ground crew helped
her put her space suit on.

Suddenly he said, 'Oh no!'

Bleurg!
He was sick all over Spacegirl's
space boots.

Mummy Neenee got some tissues
and wiped them clean.

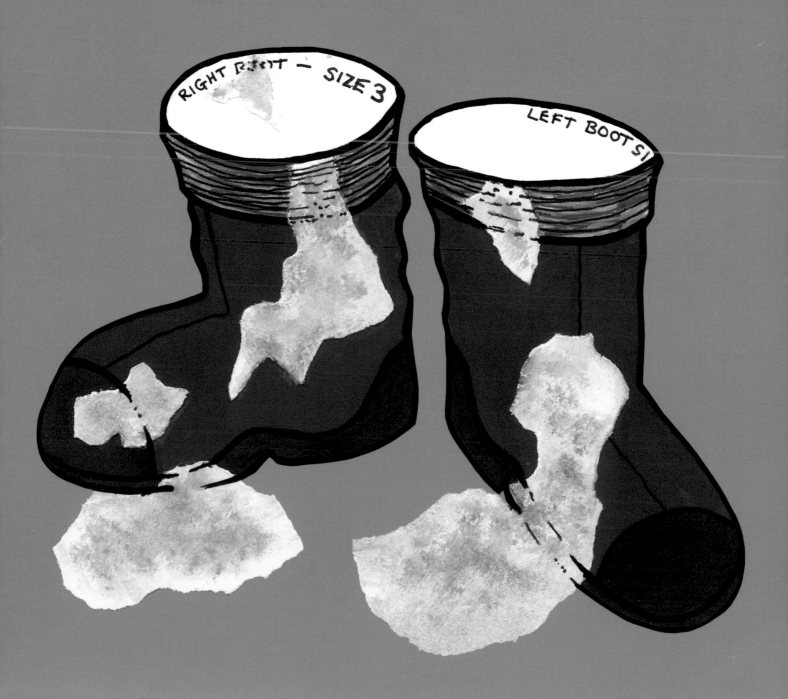

Mummy Loula and Mummy Neenee hugged Spacegirl and kissed her goodbye.

Mwah! Mwah!

Everyone counted down.
'Three, two, one, blast off!'

But the rocket didn't move.

'Is the rocket feeling ill?'
Spacegirl asked.

The ground crew all scratched their heads. Then Mummy Loula saw a little red light on the control panel.

'This rocket's got no petrol!' she said.

A crewman filled the spaceship up
with petrol from a long hose.

The mummies hugged Spacegirl
again and kissed her goodbye.

Mwah! Mwah!

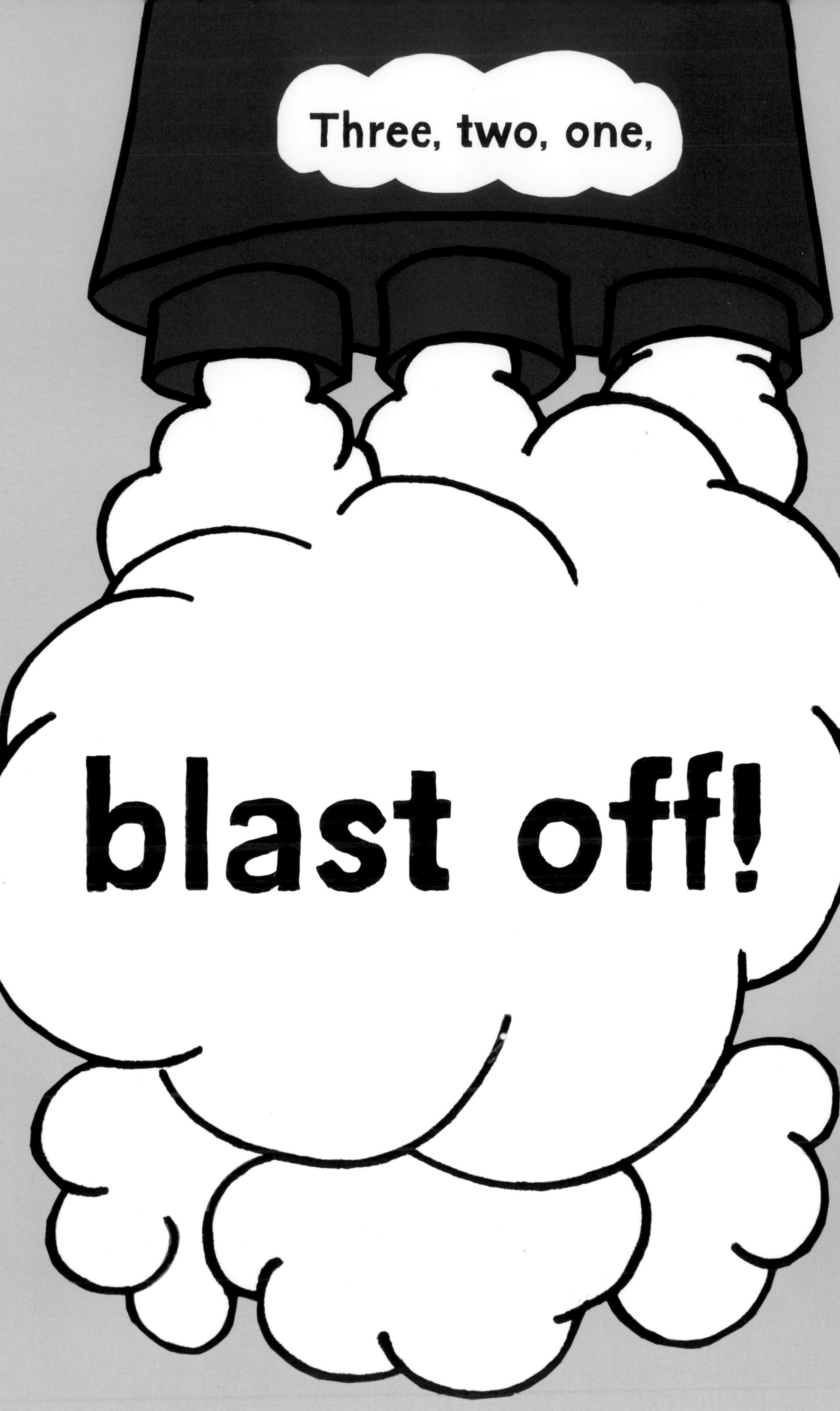
Three, two, one,
blast off!

The engines went vroom!

Spacegirl was
headed for
the stars.